IT HAPPENED AT SCHOOL

IT HAPPENED AT SCHOOL

SCHOOL

• TWO TALES •

SUSIE MORGENSTERN

illustrated by SERGE BLOCH

translated by GILLIAN ROSNER

VIKING

VIKING
Published by Penguin Group
Penguin Young Readers Group, 345 Hudson Street, New York, New York 10014, U.S.A.
Penguin Group (Canada), 10 Alcorn Avenue, Toronto, Ontario, Canada M4V 3B2
(a division of Pearson Penguin Canada Inc.)
Penguin Books Ltd, 80 Strand, London WC2R 0RL, England
Penguin Ireland, 25 St Stephen's Green, Dublin 2, Ireland (a division of Penguin Books Ltd)
Penguin Group (Australia), 250 Camberwell Road, Camberwell, Victoria 3124, Australia
(a division of Pearson Australia Group Pty Ltd)
Penguin Books India Pvt Ltd, 11 Community Centre, Panchsheel Park, New Delhi – 110 017, India
Penguin Group (NZ), Cnr Airborne and Rosedale Roads, Albany, Auckland, New Zealand
(a division of Pearson New Zealand Ltd)
Penguin Books (South Africa) (Pty) Ltd, 24 Sturdee Avenue, Rosebank,
Johannesburg 2196, South Africa

Penguin Books Ltd, Registered Offices: 80 Strand, London WC2R 0RL, England

Le fiancé de la maîtresse first published in France by l'école des loisirs, 1997
L'autographe first published in France by l'école des loisirs, 2003
First published in the United States of America in 2005 by Viking,
a division of Penguin Young Readers Group

1 3 5 7 9 10 8 6 4 2

Le fiancé de la maîtresse copyright © l'école des loisirs, Paris, 1997
L'autographe copyright © l'école des loisirs, Paris, 2003
Illustrations copyright © Serge Bloch, 2005
Translation copyright © Penguin Young Readers Group, 2005
Translation by Gillian Rosner and Jill Davis
All rights reserved

LIBRARY OF CONGRESS CATALOGING-IN-PUBLICATION DATA
Morgenstern, Susie Hoch.
[Fiancé de la maîtresse. English]
It happened at school : two tales / written by Susie Morgenstern ;
illustrated by Serge Bloch ; translated by Gillian Rosner.
p.   cm.
Two stories originally published separately in French under titles:
Le fiancé de la maîtresse and L'autographe.
Summary: In the first of two school stories set in France, a homework assignment involving
autographs has everyone excited in Claudette's class; and in the second, the persistent boyfriend of Julien's
teacher becomes a nuisance when he uses the class's new telephone/fax machine to express his love.
ISBN 0-670-06022-4 (hardcover)
1. Children's stories, French—Translations into English. 2. Schools—Juvenile fiction.
[1. Schools—Fiction. 2. Teachers—Fiction. 3. Love—Fiction. 4. Autographs—Fiction.
5. France—Fiction. 6. Humorous stories.] I. Bloch, Serge, ill. II. Rosner, Gillian, 1949–
III. Morgenstern, Susie Hoch. Autographe. English. IV. Title.
PZ7.M826714Is 2005
[Fic]—dc22
2004023695

Printed in U.S.A.
Set in Espirit
Book design by Kelley McIntyre

In memory of my mother,
Sylvia Needelman Hoch, who wrote
her autograph on my heart.
—S. M.

CONTENTS

IT HAPPENED AT SCHOOL

THE AUTOGRAPH

It was nothing more than a little piece of crumpled paper, but it was the most important thing Claudette had. Scribbled on it was the name *Rostropovich*, and it had been signed by the great musician's very own hand—the same hand that held the bow that played his beautiful cello.

Claudette played the cello, too. She listened to Rostropovich's CDs every day. One night when she had gone with her grandmother to hear a concert given by Mr. Rostropovich, she waited at his dressing room door, and the great maestro signed his name on the piece of paper she held out for him. Claudette had tenderly placed the autograph among the other keep-sakes in her scrapbook.

When their teacher, Mademoiselle Dupont, had asked her students to bring the object they valued most to school, Claudette didn't have to think twice before putting the trea-sured autograph into her school bag.

The next day, Mademoiselle Dupont's students all brought in boxes, folders, and bags holding their most precious possession and each got ready to explain why it was so important.

Xavier held up his teddy bear, saying, "I can't sleep without him!"

Frederick pulled out his house key, which was strung around his neck, saying, "Without a house, I'd be a homeless person, wandering the streets."

Holding a baguette of French bread, Sophie said, "This is a healthy way to start my day!"

Nicolas set off the buzzer to his alarm clock. He said that's what made him jump out of bed in the morning and get to school on time.

Pierre showed his PlayStation 2. "It was my favorite Christmas present!"

Sebastian took off his glasses and then put

them back on. "Thanks to these, I can see!"

Helene revealed the king from her chess set. "I am training to be a chess champion."

Not only did Alexander have the guts to bring in his ratty old blankie, but he even did a little demonstration, winding it around his fingers and then rubbing it against his cheek.

José took off the gold pendant from his neck: it was a tiny map of Corsica.

"This is my country," he announced proudly.

Jeremy caused quite a commotion. Everyone was surprised and delighted when he let his dog loose from a secret hiding place. "This is Poochini! He can sing! Really!" Jeremy started singing "Happy Birthday" at the top of his lungs while Poochini joined in with howls.

The teacher didn't know how to respond— could a dog count as an object?

Right after Poochini's performance, it was Claudette's turn. She was sure that no one else's object would compare to hers. All the others could have been bought at a store.

"Perfect timing," said Claudette. "Poochini gave a great musical performance, but I'm going to introduce you to a real live musician!"

Then she took out her crumpled piece of paper. "This page has been touched by the hand of a true genius," said Claudette. But the other students didn't seem all that impressed. In fact, they were much more impressed by the next object, which was Claire's: a bar of chocolate.

At recess, everyone started calling Claudette "Ros-tro-po-vich." She wondered whether she should have brought her cello to school instead of the autograph. She felt like an impostor when they called her Rostropovich.

The only person who seemed to appreciate Claudette's object was her teacher. The other kids just avoided her, except for chanting the four syllables of her new nickname.

The next day, Jeremy went up and whispered something into the teacher's ear.

Then Mademoiselle Dupont made an announcement: "Jeremy is sorry he decided to bring in his dog yesterday. He wants to show you something else."

Jeremy—always the performer—got up and dramatically ripped a scrap of paper from his shirt pocket. It looked just like Claudette's, and was just as crumpled. On it was written the name *Michel Ocelot*.

"Do you know," asked Jeremy, "who Michel Ocelot is?"

Nobody did.

"Well then, my clueless friends, do you at least know who Kirikou is?"

Everybody knew about the brave little boy who was the hero of a famous French animated movie.

"Michel Ocelot was the director of *Kirikou and the Sorceress*. And this piece of paper"— Jeremy gave Claudette a mean, mocking look— "has been touched by *that* hand of a genius."

Copycat, thought Claudette. *He's just a jerk—and a copycat!*

And that wasn't the end of it. Claudette soon realized that she had started a fad, because all the other kids, even ones who weren't in Claudette's class, began to litter the playground with autographs every single day. Sebastian brought in the best one of all, completely illegible, but according to Sebastian, "touched by the hand of a genius." It was the autograph of Zinédine Zidane—Zizou to his friends—the most famous soccer player in France and maybe even the whole world.

The teacher didn't think it was very likely that Sebastian had met such a big star. Sebastian finally admitted he'd gotten the autograph from his uncle, who was a sports writer.

When Monique brought in the autograph of Charlemagne, the great medieval emperor, the teacher finally lost it. But when Mademoiselle Dupont lost it, she didn't scream and yell. She spoke very quietly. She told the students to get up and come to her desk, and this is what she told them:

"Listen, Monique. Charlemagne has been dead for over a thousand years. In those days, they didn't have ballpoint pens or construction paper. They didn't have television either, and people certainly did *not* sign autographs for collectors."

"What about Rostropovich?" asked Jeremy.

"Rostropovich is still alive," replied Mademoiselle Dupont. "And your parents probably have some of his CDs.

"Come to think of it, Monique has given me an idea. I would like you all to come up with an autograph from a person you wish you could have met. Obviously it won't be a real autograph. But each of you will explain why you chose the person you did, and then you can tell us about their life."

"Mademoiselle Dupont?" asked Claudette. "Will I be able to use my Rostropovich autograph for this assignment, too?"

"Good question, Claudette. I'd prefer it if you to came in with the autograph of someone who's no longer alive. That way, we can avoid movie stars, athletes, television stars, and teen idols of the moment. I'll give you all one week to find your big hero."

For José, it was a no-brainer. Instead of his map of Corsica, he chose Napoleon Bonaparte.

This was probably because Napoleon was the only person he could think of.

Julie also had an idea—someone who was still a huge international star—even if he was dead. She decided to choose Jesus. Wasn't he the one who said, "Where your treasure is, there will your heart be also"? What a cool thing to say!

"And you, Mademoiselle Dupont, who are you going to choose?" asked Jeremy.

Teachers don't always have to answer their own questions; in fact, Mademoiselle Dupont realized she wasn't sure. Of all the men and women who had ever lived, breathed, walked, spoken, aged—who *would* Mademoiselle Dupont choose? It would probably be a writer because she loved to read. But whom did she love to read the most? Shakespeare! Yes of course, Shakespeare would be her choice.

"I'll tell you tomorrow," said Mademoiselle Dupont.

. . . . . .

If she couldn't use Rostropovich, Claudette had absolutely no idea who to choose. Maybe one of the many kings of France named Louis? Or Joan of Arc? Not too many women to choose from, it seemed. Or Mozart, maybe, but the others might think she was showing off by bringing in another musician.

In the end, the only heroes and heroines the students could think of were historical figures, the stars of history, such as Alexander the Great or Christopher Columbus.

The object that Xavier had really wanted to bring in to show everyone was his bed. But he couldn't carry it by himself. Maybe his hero could be the person who invented the bed! But what if the inventor was a caveman?

Some guy with no name? Well, he'd just have to invent the inventor himself!

Pierre had the same kind of idea, but *he* wanted to find out who the inventor of the PlayStation was. For that matter, who invented the television? And what about the computer? That was definitely the type of autograph Pierre wanted, because what would life be like without these essential items?

All the parents had a lot to say about their children's research projects as well. Alexander's father was furious. (Mr. Yeller lived up to his name!)

"How can they expect these kids to know?" Mr. Yeller asked his wife. "There they go again, giving the parents homework. As if we don't have enough work already! Now we have to do our children's homework? Just pick Victor Hugo!"

Osman's parents opted for Ataturk, the founder of the Turkish Republic.

Nicolas's folks wanted Albert Camus, the famous writer.

Claude's mom and dad voted for Asterix the Gaul, the star of a French comic strip.

Karima's parents didn't hesitate. It would have to be Muhammad.

Everyone was trying to come up with the best idea and to do the best job.

There was one Gandhi and one Gustave Eiffel, the designer of the Eiffel Tower. Claire picked Princess Diana of England.

"I was thinking of picking a great English writer, William Shakespeare, but I had another idea. I'll tell you about it when the time comes next week," Mademoiselle Dupont told the class.

Then Sebastian came to school with a note from his dad, who was a lawyer. "It's illegal and immoral to ask children to commit forgery. It's a crime!"

Mademoiselle Dupont turned red. "I am

sorry, but I don't consider it illegal to ask my students to research heroes and heroines whose lives are exemplary and who have contributed to humanity."

She was discouraged. Each and every time she tried something that was the least bit different, she was criticized and had to fight about it. Wasn't it exhausting enough to get up every morning of the week and face the twenty-six children in her class, with their twenty-six different personalities?

"What makes a man or woman admirable?" she asked.

"If we admire them!" responded Sebastian.

"Yes, but why?"

16

"Because they did something good, like Napoleon!" said José.

"Yes, but what kind of thing?"

"Well," said José, "they thought big."

"What does it mean to think big?"

"It's to want more . . . more than life gives you," said Alexander.

"It's not being lazy!" said Pierre.

"It means having fire inside of you!" said Claudette.

"Fire inside you?"

"Yes, a passion, just like Rostropovich. Instead of playing video games or watching TV, he practices his cello," said Claudette (who always complained bitterly when her mother said, "Go practice your cello!").

Would she have the passion to be a Rostropovich?

"Who in here is passionate about something?" asked Mademoiselle Dupont.

"I am!" said just about everyone.

"Tell us what it is."

"Soccer!" cried Pierre.

"Okay, yes, soccer. You're not the only one!"

"Mine's dancing," said Claire.

"TV!" said Nicolas, happy to have come up with something. "My passion is the remote control."

"But Nicolas, the remote control? Has this invention truly benefited humanity?"

"Yes, it has."

"How?"

"Because every time someone feels happy, that contributes to humanity. If every human being were happy, the world would be a happy place, wouldn't it? That's what my grandma told me."

"But is happiness the most important thing in life? Do you think that every admirable man and woman was necessarily happy?"

"No," said Claudette. "Mostly they were unhappy, and *that's* why they wanted to fix things and change the world. Just like during the French Revolution!"

"Then in order to be admirable, you have to be unhappy?" asked Nicolas.

"Or dead!" said Alexander.

"But they had their happy moments, too," added Claudette. "Like when they became famous!"

"You have to be ambitious," said Jeremy.

"And what does that mean?"

"It's bad," said Xavier.

"Why is it bad?"

No one said anything.

"It's good to be happy with what you have. Every time I want a new toy, my mom tells me that I have enough toys, and that I should just be happy with what I've got," said Claire.

"Would you be happy with what you had if you were a slave?" asked Mademoiselle Dupont.

"Or poor?"

"And if you didn't have a Game Boy?"

"And nothing to eat?"

"You see," Mademoiselle Dupont interrupted, "it's not so easy. Something good can turn into something bad, and something bad can turn into something good. One thing's for sure, though—the people we admire the most are the ones who are passionate. The one thing I wish for all of you is that you live your lives with passion!"

Nicolas wondered if there was passion in the way he zapped the remote control.

"Who did you pick?" Jeremy asked Claudette.

"I still don't know," she lied. "What about you?"

"Oh, I haven't decided yet."

Everyone was hiding their answers, afraid that the others might try to steal their hero. So each student was busy secretly planning their presentation.

Jeremy began organizing a stack of white paper. He had his own idea. It was nothing like what the teacher had asked for, but it was a really ingenious idea. A genius—that's someone who takes risks.

The week was almost over. It was the last day of the presentations, and up until now nothing too surprising had happened. Almost everyone had picked someone who was probably on a "Top 50 People of All Time" list. Xavier, for instance, chose Albert Einstein.

"And do you know what?" he asked everyone. "Do you remember when we were talking about happiness? Well, Albert Einstein once said that happiness is a good goal if you're a cow."

By the time Claudette's turn came, her classmates had heard more than enough about culture and science. But when Claudette spoke, she spoke from the heart (and not *by heart*), so everyone found it easy to listen. She held her piece of paper in the air and showed them how she'd dipped her hand in ink and stamped it on the paper, like a fingerprint.

"This is the autograph of the first man or woman who ever lived. You've got to realize what this means. It was very, very hard to be the first! The first man and woman fought hard every day just to survive: feed themselves, protect themselves, and then figure out how to keep our species going so it wouldn't end with them! I mean, having babies is the best invention of all time!"

Everyone laughed.

"But each baby born has to start this all over—making its own way, always trying to add a little something that matters to the world. Each man or woman continues the work of those who have come before and even tries to go further. Everyone in the beginning is just a twinkle in the sky."

Claudette held up her handprint once again and said, "This, therefore, is the autograph of the first person and of all the men and women who followed. It's not just my autograph, but all of ours, since we all came from the first man and woman. That's why, this time, I can declare this to be the hand of a genius."

The teacher was proud of her student.

But Jeremy felt kind of dumb after Claudette's presentation, because now it was his turn, and once again, this time without knowing it, he had more or less copied. He took out his big stack of white paper. He had gone from door to door in his neighborhood, collecting autographs from all of the store owners and neighbors. There was Renée, a hair stylist; Christine Zirk, a potter; Michel Reutter, a dentist; Christian Morrisse, a jeweler; Marcel Saule, a carpenter; Beatrice Decroix, an editor; Baptiste Affouard, a student; and Philippe Gauthier, unemployed.

"There's still one more autograph I'd like for my collection," he said, and he handed a piece of paper to Mademoiselle Dupont. After she signed, he wrote, "Teacher."

"These are real people. And we can admire them because they do what they can in life. They live. They say hello. They try not to bother anyone. They work. They eat. They have fun. They cry, too.

And even though they aren't dead now, they are still the ones I chose."

How moving and different from the others the last two presentations were, thought Mademoiselle Dupont.

"I didn't do exactly what you told us to do, either, Mademoiselle Dupont," said Alexander.

He showed her the autograph he'd chosen.

"My parents wanted it to be Victor Hugo, but I felt bad pretending that's who I admired. I never knew him, and I've never read any of his books. I've only seen the animated version of *The Hunchback of Notre Dame.* And I didn't want to forge his signature anyway, because my dad says it's illegal. So that's why I've picked someone I know very well, and it's really the only autograph I have any right to sign."

His autograph was his own name: Alexander Yeller.

"Okay, so I'm not dead, but I can guarantee you that one day I will be. By that time, I hope my name will have some honor associated with it, and that someone will want *my* autograph."

Mademoiselle Dupont's heart was filled with happiness. She couldn't believe how smart and terrific her students were.

She was so thrilled that the next day Mademoiselle Dupont gave each student an official autograph book.

"Why not start by collecting all of your friends' autographs? That way, you'll be able to remember their names for the rest of your lives. But an autograph alone is not enough. You should also write something about the person next to their autograph."

During recess, everyone was signing autographs. Jeremy wrote in Claudette's autograph book:

You are nice, I like you, but
Not as much as my sweet old mutt.

After recess, Alexander remembered that the teacher hadn't made her presentation yet.

"So what about you, Mademoiselle Dupont?"

"None of you know this," she answered, "but I lost my mom this year. She died. She was an exceptional and wonderful mother. Her passion for life began each day when the sun rose. Every time I asked her how things were going, she'd say, 'I am alive!' She gave me life, and for that I will never be able to thank her enough. She's the one who gave me my love of life. Here is her autograph."

All of the children clapped.

· · · · · ·

At the end of the day, Claudette took Jeremy's autograph book and wrote:

God created the rivers,
God created the lakes.
God created you, Jeremy,
But even God makes mistakes!

Then she signed it.

Our Teacher's ♡ Boyfriend

From the moment it arrived, I knew that this telephone/fax machine would bring us nothing but trouble. The technicians finally unraveled all their wires. They finished installing it and announced with a glow of self-satisfaction, "That's it! Puycornet School is connected!"

MONDAY

Although she never even asked for it, our teacher is delighted with this new high-tech device. It makes her feel safe. No longer is she all alone in this tiny country school with her class of twenty-two students, of whom I, Julien, am one. (Of course, she wasn't really alone—there is another class next door, taught by Mademoiselle Laurent.) Our teacher is also the school principal. Her name is Catherine Raysun, and she truly is a ray of sunshine. She's tall, youngish, thin, pretty, and best of all, she smiles a lot. But she also knows how to yell. Especially her favorite expression: "You've gone too far!"

Puycornet School may be tiny, but we have a huge classroom. So here we are, reading quietly, more or less, while Mademoiselle Raysun sits at her desk looking at the instructions for the telephone/fax machine. Suddenly, like an egg timer going off, the phone rings for the first time. *Ring ring.* It takes seven rings before the teacher realizes that the phone is now part of the classroom. She walks over to answer it.

"Puycornet School," Mademoiselle Raysun says nervously.

. . .

"Ah, it's you! You scared me."

. . .

"Yes, it *is* the right number . . . that's why *I* answered."

. . .

"Yes, okay, bye!"

No sooner is she back at her desk, than the phone rings again.

She listens. "Yes Maurice, yes," she says in a low voice.

. . .

"But of course I love you Maurice." She is whispering, but we can't help eavesdropping.

. . .

"I *do* love you." She says this a little louder. She keeps listening, frowns, and then almost angrily hisses into the receiver, "I promise I love you. I have to go."

. . .

"Yes, yes Maurice. See you tonight."

Five minutes later the fax starts buzzing, and a page pops up out of the machine like a piece of bread from the toaster. We all get up together to go see. The page is covered with hearts of all shapes and sizes. In the middle of this decorative love toast is written:

I love you by night,
I love you by day.
It's such a simple
thing to say.
And so I simply have
to say,
Hello my love,
by night and by day.

Catherine
+
Maurice

Our teacher rips the paper from the machine, crumples it up, and stuffs it into her purse. Then she throws herself into teaching us our math lesson. She gives us a problem that is hard yet fun; that's the way I like them! She tries to work out the answer while we do, saying, "The first one to get it wins!"

"Wins what?" asks Serge.

"My undying admiration."

Personally, whether we win admiration, money, or even candy, it's all the same to me. Finding the answer to a problem is only half the fun: the other half is looking for it. Still, winning is always good, and that's what I want right now. I solve the problem as fast as I can, and just as fast, I raise my hand.

But before anyone can notice that I've actually won, that *ring ring* starts again, and our teacher jumps up to answer the phone.

"Puycornet School."

· · ·

"Oh . . . it's you again. . . . Did you forget to say something important?"

. . .

"I know, Maurice," she snaps. "You've already told me three hundred and eighty times. Once a day is plenty."

She is listening to him impatiently, standing on one leg, then the other.

"Yes Maurice. You already know that. I'm not saying it again."

. . .

"Okay Maurice. For the last time! I love you."

The trouble with the telephone is that you only hear one half of the conversation. Just for fun, I find myself whispering what I think that silly Maurice must be saying. His vocabulary is boring, just like he is. He only knows three words. *I love you. I love you. I love you.*

Maybe Maurice isn't even a man: maybe he's a parrot. *I love you. I love you.* Does he have the faintest idea of what that means? Personally, I have never actually *said* it to anyone, but I suppose I *think* it about people like Grandma, Mom, our teacher, and maybe even Naomi Vacquier.

Naomi is the smartest girl in the class, and she's the nicest, too. I've noticed that the smartest ones are often the nicest. Maybe they can afford to be that way because they have fewer problems in life. They have time to smile and be friendly. Beatrice Lefebre is the complete opposite. When you ask her a question like "What are we supposed to be doing?" or a favor like "Can I borrow your eraser?" she pretends not to hear. I know this, because it is my bad luck to have to sit next to her. Of course Naomi Vacquier sits on the other side of the classroom.

By the time a few more *I love you*s are said,

the whole class has had forever to solve the problem. Every finger of every hand is waving in the air. How can our teacher possibly know that mine was first? Out of the two hundred and twenty fingers, Mademoiselle Raysun makes the mistake of calling on Beatrice Lefebre. This is probably because as well as waving her fingers, Beatrice is also screaming hysterically, "Me! Call on me!" Plus, Mademoiselle Raysun has no idea that Beatrice Lefebre has copied everything from my book! So Beatrice has managed to get on Mademoiselle Raysun's good side and on my bad side at the exact same time. Although in fact, she's already been on my bad side for a long time. But what does she care?

Still, Beatrice does come in handy from time to time. . . . For example, she is my clock. When she gets her snack out of her bag, I know it's ten o'clock and time for recess. Beatrice has the best snacks in the class, because her father is a baker. Of course, it

would never cross her mind to share; she does the complete opposite: she runs to a corner of the playground where she can stuff herself with her golden brioche in private.

But on this historic occasion, the day of the telephone/fax, our teacher completely forgets about recess. Beatrice's fingers search for her snack and remind me I'm hungry. I can't think about work, friends, or anything else, and I'm relieved when finally Mademoiselle Raysun announces it's lunchtime.

We get up from our seats as we have been

41

taught: quietly and in an orderly fashion. I worry that everyone can hear my stomach rumbling. I read the menu and see we're having grilled cheese. If I don't get a bite immediately, I may end up biting Beatrice Lefebre. The smell of melting cheese wafts up from the kitchen. Madame Ferrari is a good cook. The teacher is about to open the classroom door. I hear Madame Ferrari shout, *"Andiamo ragazzi,* let's go kids, it's ready!" The delicious smell is killing me. Mademoiselle Raysun doesn't need to give us her usual "I'm waiting for absolute silence," because we're already so quiet you can hear birds chirping and leaves rustling outside. *"Andiamo,"* I say to myself. But the telephone says the opposite. *Ring ring, ring ring.*

Our teacher turns around and pushes us out of the way. After six rings she grabs the phone.

I can tell from her expression that it's Maurice again. I can also tell you that life sometimes spins out of control. Take things like belches and gas that bubble up from within. Or worse, vomit! Once I even threw up in front of the whole class. There's nothing you can do about these things; they are like volcanic eruptions. But today it is much worse: today I have a verbal eruption!

Before the teacher can say it for herself, I yell out uncontrollably, "Yes of course Maurice, I looooove you!"

What a shock. Mademoiselle Raysun blushes from head to toe. Funnily enough, though, she isn't annoyed with me, but with that guy on the other end of the line. She listens to him, looking bored out of her mind, then announces firmly, "Maurice, I'm telling you for the last time: I love you. But you've gone too far! Don't you dare call me again today. Can't you understand? I'm working!"

The grilled cheese is cold and soggy. The

cafeteria is hot and noisy. Mademoiselle Ray-sun is stressed out and exhausted.

And that is how the telephone/fax brought Maurice into our class. He was quiet all afternoon, but we could feel his presence lurking. Maurice became the ghost of Puycornet School.

TUESDAY

All night long I tried to imagine what Maurice looked like. But instead of eyes, I saw *I love you*s, and it was the same for his nose and mouth.

"What do you think Maurice looks like?" I ask Naomi the next day.

"He's tall and looks smart," she replies.

"He's blond with blue eyes," adds Alexis, who has dark hair and brown eyes.

"He looks like a movie star," sighs Eloise.

"He's skinny," says Beatrice, who is fat.

"Do you think he's a school principal?"

"No, he's probably a doctor."

"Or a lawyer."

"He must be pretty rich," said Alexis.

"He's really nice," adds Naomi.

He seems like a fool, I think to myself, *but I suppose if our teacher loves him, he must be handsome—and a good guy.*

But this morning the good guy does not get off to a good start.

Mademoiselle Raysun announces that we'll begin with P.E. while it's still sunny outside, because the weatherman said it's going to be rainy later. Everyone except that pill Beatrice is happy.

Our teacher says she wants to teach us a new ball game. As everyone knows, the ball is definitely one of mankind's greatest inventions. Without the ball there would be no soccer, no football, no basketball—not even tennis. As our teacher gets a ball from the closet, we are side-tracked by the sound of one of the world's worst inventions: *ring ring, ring ring*. Mademoiselle Raysun rushes toward the phone to comfort that whiner on the other end. At the same time, she makes the mistake of throwing the ball to Ludovic, who hugs it to his chest like a teddy bear.

"Puycornet School," she answers in her teacher's voice.

Then in a sweet voice she whispers, "Maurice."

. . .

"Yes, yes, me too."

Ludovic raises the ball to his face and kisses it all over. *Smack!* "Maurice, kiss me, kiss me Maurice. Kiss me a hundred times. Oh Maurice! Maurice!

More! Kiss me again, Maurice."

After he is through with this love scene, Ludovic throws the ball to Gregory, who acts out his own version before throwing the ball to Eloise. She tosses it into the air. It lands on the teacher's table, right on a vase of tulips. The vase breaks, water runs over all our papers (our tests from last week!), and the flowers cascade to the floor.

"I have to go Maurice."

Catastrophe!

"Yes, Maurice, I do love you."

She hangs up saying, "That's it! You've gone too far! Go back to your seats! No P.E. today. Give me back that ball. Look at this mess! These tests you took are soaking wet. Now you'll have to take another one."

Our teacher is very well organized. She has already written all the tests until the end of the year. She's really mad: gone are her favorite springtime tulips and the one and only classroom vase. She doesn't usually like to punish us, but she also doesn't like to go back on her word, so she hands out the papers for the test we should have had at the end of the year. We don't know any of the answers, and it's depressing!

Naomi Vacquier bursts into tears. We see our teacher feels bad for us. She assures us that these grades won't count. "I'm going to explain the answers."

Our curiosity makes us pay attention. Mademoiselle Raysun goes to the blackboard and starts writing the answer to question number one. Forty-four eyes are glued to the chalk going up and down as half a word appears. So far it looks like I got the right answer. But I'm not sure yet, and before she can finish the word, there goes Mr. Ring Ring! Our teacher looks annoyed. "Answer it, Julien," she tells me, realizing that she is not the only one who can.

I pick up the receiver and copy her: "Puycornet School." And I add, "At your service."

The caller (it must be *him*!) asks for Mademoiselle Raysun, and I decide to answer for her.

"Mademoiselle Raysun can't come to the phone right now. Can I take a message?"

. . .

"Yes. Thank you. I'll give her your message."

I am the perfect secretary. One day I went with my aunt to her office, where she spent all day answering the phone just like this.

Mademoiselle Raysun looks at me and raises an eyebrow. That's her way of asking a question. I reply, trying not to laugh, "It was Maurice. The message is: 'Tell Catherine that I love her.'" I tried to imitate his musical, deep, TV-announcer's voice, but our teacher doesn't laugh.

It's funny. Last week, or even two days ago, we didn't know who Maurice *was*. Now he takes up all our time!

When the phone rings again, Mademoiselle

Raysun says, "Nobody answer it. We'll just let it ring."

Ludovic counts out loud: "One, two, three, four, five, six, seven . . ." up to thirty-nine, before it stops.

And it goes on: every five minutes, the phone blares out for at least three rings. It's so annoying! The only thing we can think about is that awful telephone that is either ringing or just about to. Finally, Mademoiselle Raysun decides to take it off the hook. And now in the background, we hear the buzz of a never-ending dial tone. From where I sit, right next to the monster, it's just miserable.

Naomi, whose parents are both doctors, suggests to our teacher that she buy an answering machine, so the caller can leave a message.

Alexis shouts, "Yes," and continues in his robot voice: "You-have-reached-Puycornet-School. We-are-sorry-we-cannot-talk-to-you-at-this-time-but-we-are-in-the-middle-of-class.

Please-leave-a-message-after-the-beep-and-we'll-get-back-to-you-as-soon-as-possible."

Mademoiselle Raysun smiles despite her annoyance. Maybe she's thinking of the miles of tape in the machine that would have one message repeated over and over: *I love you, I love you, I love you.* Big deal! Saying "I love you" costs nothing, and if you say it too often, it means nothing, too.

"No," our teacher says seriously. "That's enough with machines. We have too many already." Perplexed, she stares at the telephone/fax and forcefully unplugs it, repeating, "That's enough."

Finally! The classroom returns to normal. Our teacher is humming happily as she writes the test answers on the board.

This calm scene is loudly interrupted a while later by a knocking on the door followed by someone rushing quickly into the classroom. It is the Mayor of Puycornet herself, and she does not look happy. This is when we realize that we can't simply throw away this new telephone/fax machine!

"Catherine," the mayor blurts out hurriedly, "I've been trying to call you. Come quickly!"

Our teacher leaves the room with the mayor. The mayor of our village is not exactly the president of the country—she's only the mayor, and also the mother of our classmate, Nadine Desplats. According to my father, she doesn't even belong to a political party. She only wants to do some good for our village, and—still according to my father—she does a good job, because after all she has managed to save our school when they wanted to close it and send us all to different schools in neighboring villages.

Through the window we stare at the two of them talking, but unfortunately we can't hear a word they say. Watching them, I realize

what I want to be when I'm older: I want to be a spy so I can listen to everyone's conversations. I'm fascinated by what people say to each other. I'm sure the mayor has come to deliver Mademoiselle Raysun an urgent message from Maurice: "Catherine, Maurice loves you."

Mademoiselle Raysun comes back into class looking serious. She goes next door and tells the other teacher that she has to leave and asks her to keep an eye on us. Then she walks toward me with the saddest look on her face. I am terrified. I think there must have been an accident: my mother, my father, my big brother. When she reaches my seat, she turns her head and looks at Beatrice Lefebre.

"Your mother called the town hall. There is a small problem. I'm taking you home."

Beatrice says nothing. She stands up and holds our teacher's hand. But she doesn't forget to take her brioche from its hiding place. At the door, the teacher quickly walks back to my side of the room, reconnects the telephone/ fax, and tells us to do some silent reading. We don't even try to do anything else.

Beatrice's empty seat gives me the chills. She's not exactly my friend, but she does fill a spot in my life. I'm used to having her there picking up the crumbs from her brioche, then picking up the answers off my paper.

The class is silent. We are sitting as still as statues. This time, when the phone rings we are happy about it. Since I am the closest, I answer it in my most professional voice: "Puycornet School."

Of course it's Maurice. But this deceivingly nice voice has the nerve to complain to *me*: he's been trying to call for hours, he has something urgent to say to Catherine, but since nothing ever works in this country . . . ! It's as if I were personally responsible. What's worse, I already know what he wants to say to our teacher. I'd like to warn him, man to man, that he is ruining his chances with his constant *I love you*s. But I say nothing, except that our teacher is not in.

Mademoiselle Raysun has just gotten back, when the fax machine buzzes to tell us we are about to get its opinion. From my seat, I can see the huge letters:

I know it makes you scream
but I can't help what I do,
And even in my dreams
I repeat that I love you, I love you, I love you. . . .

OUR TEACHER'S BOYFRIEND

Our teacher is so overwhelmed by us, the fax, and the problem with Beatrice that she doesn't even bother to pick up her fax. She leaves it there for everyone to see, and tells us that Beatrice's father has been in an accident at work and has been taken to Montauban Hospital. He is in good hands and will probably be better soon. Beatrice is keeping her mother company.

Although our teacher isn't the forgetful type, she totally forgets to go on with the answers to the test. She also forgets that she had decided to take away our P.E. time today, and goes to get the ball from the closet.

"Get in line," she says while holding the ball. We are happy finally to be outside, to get into a circle, and to listen to the rules of the game. Only now, the raindrops begin to fall harder and harder. . . .

Mademoiselle Raysun doesn't know what to do with us. She sits on her desk and stares into space like a machine that has broken down. But the other machine has definitely not broken down because it continues its *ring ring*. Our teacher gets up slowly with a look that could kill. She grabs the receiver like a gun fighter, opens her mouth, and yells: "That's enough! You've gone too far."

. . .

"Department of Education? Oh, excuse me; I was talking to the children. . . . The superintendent is coming to observe the class? Yes . . . yes, on Friday. Fine. Three o'clock. Thank you for letting me know."

Unlike the previous calls, this one jolts our teacher like a double espresso coffee. Full of energy, she rallies us: "Now let's get down to work." And off we go on a journey through history and geography.

We make a stop in ancient Egypt. Our teacher has gotten back her usual enthusiasm and explains archaeological discoveries as though this were the dress rehearsal for the superintendent's visit.

We are in a caravan of camels winding along the banks of the Nile, about to go by a pyramid, when that Sphinx Maurice drags us back to Puycornet. Mademoiselle Raysun no longer tries to ignore the cry of the beast that has been with us since Monday. Looking worried, she answers, "Puycornet School?"

"Oh no! *Maurice*, you're getting on my nerves!"

Suddenly, she looks defeated. She's crying like she's heartbroken. Her voice changes, too.

"No, I don't love you. I no

61

longer love you! I don't want you to call me again. I don't want to see you again! You are crazy, completely crazy. You've gone too far. You are out of my life! Out! Don't you get it?"

The receiver comes crashing down on its cradle. Our teacher falls into her chair and turns away, so we can't see her tears.

And that is what high-tech communication has brought to Puycornet School.

WEDNESDAY

On Wednesday we don't have class, since it is our day off.

THURSDAY

The whites of our teacher's eyes are red and so is the tip of her nose. She has rings under her eyes, bags even, and little wrinkles. I notice these things because my mother is always asking me if *she* has them. In two days, Mademoiselle Raysun has aged ten years.

What is worse, she is completely out of it. She has lost her voice, her strength, her energy. She writes one word on the board and robotically gives us instructions. She passes out pieces of blank paper and hides behind her desk, holding her sagging head between her clammy hands. She closes her eyes.

We are supposed to write about the word on the board. Only the word she has written is "Love." We are not exactly experts on the subject.

I look around. Beatrice is still absent, so now I can see the whole class.

No one is writing.

Mademoiselle Laurent, the other teacher, tiptoes in and whispers very loudly, "Catherine, you look really awful!"

Mademoiselle Raysun stares through her as if Mademoiselle Laurent were not there.

"You know, you look like you're going to lose it. That's the last thing you need with the superintendent coming tomorrow! Here's what you're going to do: go home and rest. I'll take care of your kids for you. It's springtime. We'll go for a nature walk."

Mademoiselle Raysun gets to her feet without protesting. She hugs her colleague and leaves without saying good-bye to us.

We know Mademoiselle Laurent well, and she knows us because she was our teacher last year. She walks into the classroom saying, "Keep doing what you were doing!"

That's a lot of help! And what about the nature walk?

I write: "I love my parents. I think it's because I see them every day and because they love me, too. We are so used to each other by now we couldn't do without each other. Love is when you can't live without someone."

I'm about to begin a new section on my grandmother when a beep comes out of the fax.

It's a miracle! The fax is doing the assignment for us.

You can be crazy without being in love, but you can't be in love without being crazy!

Maurice

I don't really know what he means, except that he is crazy and has driven our teacher crazy, too.

Five minutes later, it's:

Love which cannot criticize is not love.

Maurice

SUSIE MORGENSTERN

And:

Then:

Then:

Luckily, our teacher isn't here, because she really would've gone crazy with this fax spitting out love letters every two minutes. For me, it's great, because through Maurice's words I learn that you can say whatever you want about love, even things that are completely opposite, since both could easily be true. So I write, "We live for love, and we die for love."

I look up to see Naomi Vacquier looking at me, and I write, "Love gives us a little bit of hope." I notice that now, all the others are scribbling away furiously. That's the way it always goes. A pencil is like the ignition on a car—you scratch it around on the paper over and over to get started, until finally the motor bursts to life. Then I write, "Everyone dreams of love."

Just then, Mademoiselle Laurent comes to get us for the springtime walk. I write one more sentence: "It's better to be a fool in love than not in love at all." Then I get in line behind Naomi Vacquier.

FRIDAY

We are all waiting to see if our teacher will come to school. It's no fun when she's not there, even when she's no fun herself.

I peek into the room before going in, and I'm relieved to see her standing in front of the blackboard wearing what looks like a new outfit. She must be trying to convince herself that life goes on. Anyway, it isn't her fault that Maurice is crazy.

The morning goes by without any drama. We straighten up the classroom. Maurice is being good: he's keeping quiet. Madame Ferrari makes a spicy spaghetti with garlic bread for lunch. It gives you heartburn when you eat it, but she says, "Garlic is good for lovers." I think you must really have to love someone to put up with garlic breath!

We file back into the classroom—spotlessly neat and clean for the superintendent's benefit. I say a quick prayer for the teacher, because I know how important this visit is. I also pray that Maurice doesn't decide to call or fax right in the middle of the lesson. Please

let this morning's good behavior last!

There is a knock at the door and the superintendent comes in. We stand up. We sit down. Right on cue, the fax machine starts its dreaded humming, as if it had read my thoughts, and the following message pours out:

> If we are in love, we cannot be wise: and if we are wise, we cannot be in love!
>
> Maurice

Our teacher asks the superintendent to take a seat, trying to ignore the electronic message. She is just starting the lesson when the fax machine starts up again:

> Love is a crocodile on the river of desire.
>
> Catherine + Maurice

The superintendent, who is sitting not far from me—that is, not far from the abominable fax machine—picks up the fax and reads it. She has probably never seen such an active fax machine in her life!

Our teacher is about to continue the lesson, when the fax machine comes to life again, this time with:

"God always helps madmen, drunks, and lovers."

Marguerite de Navarre,
& Maurice

I see a murderous look in our teacher's eyes. She steps toward the love machine to stop its outbursts once and for all. But just as she reaches it, another message arrives from the outside world:

"The good thing about quarreling is making up."
Alfred de Musset, & Maurice

"Are you trading faxes with another class?" asks the superintendent.

Fortunately, she is one of those people who have so much confidence that they never have to wait for a question to be answered, because their answer is already in the question. "That's

Our Teacher's Boyfriend

excellent!" she proclaims. "A true initiation to the art of communication. And so original, like modern-day pen pals! I see that you have chosen love as the theme. Excellent idea! Well done!"

Our teacher, who was just about to unplug the machine, quickly turns back around and continues the lesson.

I am the only one who is listening to her. That's the way it often goes with teachers. They talk on and on, and maybe what they say is even interesting, only it often doesn't interest us. It's hard to listen. You can try to force yourself to pay attention, but you realize you aren't hearing the words. They hang there just outside your brain, as if a customs officer is refusing to let them into some mysterious country.

Our poor teacher goes on talking while the superintendent, like us, pretends to listen. But she is more interested in the sudden

arrival of a truck honking its horn for someone to open the school gate. Madame Ferrari
opens it, and the truck driver gets out and
invades the classroom with a sweet-smelling
delivery. After he's made several trips back
and forth between the truck and the class,
our classroom looks like a flower market.

There are baskets, bouquets, pots, plants,
and a heart-shaped wreath with a label that
reads: *"I love you. Maurice."*

He must have bought a whole flower shop!

The superintendent is enchanted. After all, as well as being a superintendent, she is also a woman! Lessons never looked—or smelled—this good before!

A smaller truck parks in front of the school. The driver gets out and tries to open the gate. Then he tries climbing over it, and when that fails, he tries to jump over it. Finally, Madame Ferrari, always on the look-out, opens it and lets him in.

He unloads the trunk. Out come big shrink-wrapped packages all decorated with bows and ribbons. There are all sorts of animals: rabbits, fish, bears, and even pigs—all made out of chocolate! As if he were following some silent instructions, the delivery man places one animal in front of each of us, including the superintendent, and the empty place where Beatrice Lefebre usually sits. Next he brings in boxes—heart-shaped, obviously—and the note:

Love may be sweet, but it's even better with chocolate. Maurice

Our teacher doesn't dare look at the superintendent. In any case, she doesn't have time to, because right after the chocolate delivery, a guy we have never seen before turns up out of nowhere and makes his way to the front of the classroom.

He is shorter than our teacher, a bit fat, and bald—in fact, a little funny looking. He is wearing an enormous pair of glasses perched on the end of his nose. He's all dressed up, like my dad when he went to the opera: he's got the white shirt, the suit, and the bow tie, but something's off. He looks as if his clothes had been made for someone else, as if he's in a costume. I would never have guessed that it was *him* if our teacher hadn't yelled, "*Maurice!*" at the top of her lungs.

And I would never have imagined him like *that*: short, fat, and bald, with glasses.

What does she see in him? But I've already figured out the answer: Love is blind!

"Let's get married, Catherine!" says this weird little man.

"Go away!" our teacher whispers in reply. "I'm working!"

We are speechless, staring at Maurice standing there in front of the class, when Beatrice Lefebre comes in with her father and Madame Ferrari.

Beatrice sits quietly down beside me without saying so much as hello. Her father announces, "I'm so happy I wasn't hurt too badly in the accident that I've made a batch of giant brioches for everyone."

Another delivery man arrives, out of breath from carrying soda bottles. That's when Maurice bursts into song. What a voice for someone who's not only weird but not even handsome! It's a voice that is strong and sweet at the same time, a voice like a choir of angels. He looks at Mademoiselle Raysun and sings, "Don't leave me."

In the middle of his song, the mayor walks in and slams the door. She is dying to say something, but she, too, is rendered speechless by Maurice's voice.

At the end of the song, she says weakly, "What on earth is going on here, Catherine?"

And our teacher, moving in to hug her boyfriend, replies, "You told me your favorite task as mayor was to perform weddings. Well, get ready for ours!"

Long live the telephone!

Long live the fax!

Long live communication, school, and Puycornet!

Long live lovers!

Long live love!

Long live chocolate!